Joe Lee and the Boo

WHO'S AFRAID OF MONSTERS?

story by Ryan Jacobson
illustrations by Elizabeth Hurley

Zachary,
"Boo" to you!

2/09

GETCHU! BOOKS
an imprint of Lake 7 Creative
MORA, MINNESOTA

Acknowledgements

A very special thanks to Mike and Jacie Lemke. Without your support, this project would not have been possible. I would also like to recognize Evelyn Hughes, whose input was invaluable. Many thanks to Blake Hoena, Cheri Jacobson, Dana Kuznar, Jon Norberg, Melba Pack, Karla Schiller and countless others who have provided help along the way. Lastly, thank you to my wife, Lora, for being my everything.

—Ryan Jacobson

Special thanks to Brent Schoonover, Charlene Smith, Jennifer Hein and Tom Garrett for helping me throughout the years.

—Elizabeth Hurley

Cover typography by Shane Nitzsche

1 2 3 4 5 6 10 09 08 07 06 05

Copyright 2008 by Ryan Jacobson
Published by Getchu Books, an imprint of Lake 7 Creative
530 Park Street South
Mora, MN 55051
www.getchubooks.com

ISBN-13: 978-0-9821187-0-2
ISBN-10: 0-9821187-0-8

For Jonah (and for his pal Boo). You are my greatest joy and the source of my courage. I love you.

—Ryan Jacobson

To my true loves Keith and Gwyneth who inspire me to try every day to grow more, do more and be more.

—Elizabeth Hurley

Joe Lee Jensen had a problem. A monster was lurking inside his closet. He also had a solution. He was going to frighten that monster away.

Unfortunately, Joe Lee didn't know how to scare monsters. To be honest, monsters scared him.

He sat awake in his bedroom, only his bedroom wasn't a bedroom anymore. It was a dank, dirty swamp filled with snakes and gators and spiders.

Worst of all, the monster was coming to get him!

"Who's afraid of monsters?" said a deep, grizzly voice.

"I am," whispered Joe Lee.

He looked at his closet. Then he gazed beyond the vines and bushes and weeds, toward his bedroom door.

I'll scare that monster some other day, he decided.

Joe Lee jumped out of bed, leapt toward the door and sprang into the hallway. But the hallway wasn't a hallway anymore.

It was a giant, endless maze filled with dead ends and traps and monsters.

"Who's afraid of monsters?" said a deep, grizzly voice.

"I am," whispered Joe Lee.

He dashed through the maze, dodged the dangerous traps and darted to his parents' bedroom.

"Mom, Dad, help!"

Joe Lee dove into the bed and ducked under the warm, soft covers.

There's a monster in my closet," he told his parents.

Again?" his father asked in a sleepy voice.
I thought you were going to scare it away."

I don't know how," admitted Joe Lee.

There's no such thing as monsters,"
said his mother.

Joe Lee didn't answer.
He started to snore.

Joe Lee awakened to a cold, rainy Saturday. He wanted to play basement explorer, but he could hear the monster and its friends growling and snarling and smacking below.

Maybe monsters are scared of flashlights, he thought.

He crept down the stairs, but when he reached the bottom, the basement wasn't a basement anymore. It was a black, moldy cave filled with rats and bats and serpents.

"Who's afraid of monsters?" said a deep, grizzly voice.

"I am," whispered Joe Lee.

The monster grinned wickedly.

"Monsters aren't afraid of flashlights!" Joe Lee screamed.

He raced up the stairs, only the stairs weren't stairs anymore. They were a steep, slippery mountain slope covered with rocks and pebbles and snow.

It took all of Joe Lee's energy to scale the treacherous cliff as the monster hurried after him.

Joe Lee summited the mountain and burst into the kitchen.

"The monster is chasing me!" he cried.

"There's no such thing as monsters," said his mother.

Joe Lee did not agree. He glanced down the mountain slope, but the monster had vanished.

Maybe I don't want to be a famous basement explorer, thought Joe Lee.

Instead, he decided that he was a secret agent. The government had sent him to spy on his father.

Joe Lee followed him into the living room. He followed him into the dining room. He even followed him into the bathroom.

"Joe Lee," said his father,
"you're going to have to stay out there."

As Joe Lee waited, his mother called from
the kitchen. "Joe Lee, come quickly!"

Oh, no, thought Joe Lee. *The monster is after my mom!*

He rushed through the dining room, only the dining room wasn't a dining room anymore. It was a tall, thick forest filled with wolves and bears and owls. Worst of all, the monster was sitting at the dining room table.

"I have to keep going," Joe Lee said to himself. "Mom needs me."

But the monster wouldn't let him pass. "Who's afraid of monsters?" said a deep, grizzly voice.

"I am," whispered Joe Lee. "But I'll find out how to scare you."

In the kitchen, something barked.

"What was that?" asked the monster.

"I don't know," said Joe Lee.

The monster whimpered. "It sounded like a dog. Monsters don't like dogs."

A black and white puppy bounded into the tall, thick forest.

"Arf! Arf!" barked the puppy.

The monster screamed. It vaulted away from the table, scampered toward the trees and disappeared into the forest.

"Joe Lee," said his mother, "I have a surprise for you, but it looks like you've already met him."

The boy shook with excitement. He swooped up the dog and squeezed it tightly.

"What's his name?" asked Joe Lee.

His father peeked into the dining room, smiling. "That's for you to decide."

Joe Lee thought for a moment. "He scares monsters, so he needs a good name. I'll call him the Boo."

Joe Lee was once again a famous basement explorer, but the basement wasn't a basement anymore. It was a black, moldy cave filled with rats and bats and monsters.

"Who's afraid of monsters?" said a deep, grizzly voice.

Joe Lee did not reply.

"Who's afraid of monsters?" the voice repeated, louder than before.

"Mr. Monster," said Joe Lee. "I'd like to ask you a question."

"Well, that's never happened before," said the monster. "Go ahead."

"Who's afraid of the Boo?" said Joe Lee in his deepest, grizzliest voice.

"I am," whispered the monster.

"Then you'd better run because me and the Boo are going to get you!"

The monster retreated up the steep, slippery mountain slope. It darted through the tall, thick forest. It weaved in and out of the giant, endless maze. All the while, Joe Lee and the Boo chased it.

They finally caught up with it in Joe Lee's bedroom. The monster zoomed into the closet and slammed the door closed behind it.

That night, Joe Lee wasn't alone in his bedroom.
His best friend, the Boo, slept by his side.

The monster crouched inside Joe Lee's closet,
but it wasn't waiting to scare a little boy.

It was hiding from Joe Lee and the Boo.

QUESTIONS FOR DISCUSSION

1. Do you think Joe Lee's monster was real or imaginary? Why?

2. Do you have any pets? If so, what kind? What sorts of games do you play together?

3. Joe Lee's monster was afraid of dogs. What else do you think monsters are afraid of?

4. If a monster were in your closet, how would you frighten it away?

5. At first, Joe Lee was scared of the monster, but by the end of the story he wasn't anymore. What scares you? What can you do so you're not scared anymore?

ABOUT THE CREATORS

Ryan Jacobson has always loved monster books, so he was thrilled to get a chance to write one. He based this story on his childhood fear of snakes hiding in his bed. (It wasn't until he got a pet dog named Spunky that he overcame his fear.)

Ryan is the author of eight children's books, including a picture book, three comic books, three chapter books and a choose-your-path book. He lists writing as a favorite hobby, and he enjoys sharing his stories during elementary school visits.

The author lives in Mora, Minnesota, with his wife Lora, son Jonah and dog Boo. For more about Ryan, visit his website at www.RyanJacobsonOnline.com.

Elizabeth Hurley loves creating art for kids. *Joe Lee and the Boo: Who's Afraid of Monsters* is her second children's book, but Elizabeth also embroiders and paints murals for nurseries and kids' bedrooms.

Elizabeth grew up on various military bases but spent most of her young life doodling and drawing sketches in Seoul, Korea, and Virginia. Her love of art led her to the Minneapolis College of Art and Design, where she graduated with a Bachelor of Fine Arts Degree in Illustration.

She lives in Minneapolis, Minnesota, with her husband Keith, daughter Gwyneth and dog Boomer. For more information, visit www.ElizabethHurleyIllustrations.com.

MORE BOOKS BY RYAN JACOBSON

Santa Claus: Super Spy: The Case of the Florida Freeze

The first book in the Super Spy series introduces readers to Santa's secret life. He's a Super Spy! The jolly old man chooses two children, Paul and Emily, to join him on an exciting adventure. Together they must stop the evil Jack Frost from freezing Florida forever.

80 pages · 18 illustrations · softcover · $4.99 · ISBN-13: 978-0-9774122-0-4

Santa Claus: Super Spy: The Case of the Delaware Dinosaur

Paul and Emily are back to join Santa Claus on their second adventure. This time a giant dinosaur is loose in the state of Delaware, and it's up to the Super Spies to catch it. Are Paul and Emily brave enough? Or will they become the dinosaur's next meal?

112 pages · 22 illustrations · softcover · $4.99 · ISBN-13: 978-0-9774122-1-1

Santa Claus: Super Spy: The Case of the Colorado Cowboy

Paul Jenkins is at the Denver Rodeo, having the time of his life. But the fun doesn't last. When strange "accidents" start to happen, Paul and his new friend Cassie call Santa and Emily for help. Who's behind these dangerous attacks? Will the Super Spies solve this mystery? Or will someone get hurt?

112 pages · 20 illustrations · softcover · $4.99 · ISBN: 978-0-9774122-2-8

Order these books and more at www.RyanJacobsonOnline.com